UnRaveled

Justine-
I hope you
enjoy UnRaveled!
K. Bromberg

K. Bromberg

This book is a work of fiction. Names, characters, places, and incidents are the product of the author's imagination or are used fictitiously. Any resemblance to actual events, locales, or persons, living or dead, is coincidental.

Cover art created by **Christina Leigh Designs**
with Shutterstock image # 328880,

Copy and Line editing by **The Polished Pen**

Formatting by **Champagne Formats**

Dedication

To my V.P. Pit Crew:
Two immeasurable words:
Thank you.

Disclaimer:

Please be advised that UnRaveled is a darker erotic novella that is not suitable for people sensitive to situations dealing with sexual duress or hard to read subjects.

This is a story about a stale marriage and the couple's unconventional attempt at communication and finding that spark again.

A Note from the Author

Dear Reader:

While the subject matter in UnRaveled pushes some boundaries and blurs the edge of the moral compass…it also begs you to ask yourself questions you might have previously chosen to ignore. The story pushes you to wonder why you and your spouse have become complacent as a couple. It forces you look within yourself to see how you can be turned on by something when you know you're not supposed to be. It urges you wonder why you're not communicating your needs better within your own relationship. It makes you turn to that partner and speak up for the first time in a long time about what exactly it is that you need.

UnRaveled is a work of fiction. Sometimes in fiction authors use literary freedom to push boundaries in unconventional ways to make a point. I have done that in this short story.

I have left numerous questions unanswered for you, the reader, to fill in as you see fit. I want you to use your imagination to complete them. I want you to justify or not justify with your own mind how what occurs can be acceptable or unacceptable. Regardless of what it is, I want you to question: the story, Lilly, Anderson, and most importantly yourself.

You might not like UnRaveled. You might actually hate it and say not for me. Regardless if you do or don't, the one thing I hope you take away from it, is that it made you think.

On a final note, I understand why certain things within UnRaveled are controversial. That was not my intention. I'm not trying to be inconsiderate by any means to those that have been forced into a situation of non-consensual sex in whatever form it is.... Please know that and take that to heart.

Thank you for reading,
Kristy

Chapter 1

I WISH THAT I'd never looked up.

I wish that I'd kept my head down and focused on the ice cubes floating aimlessly in my glass, a mirror reflection of how I felt. Living one day to the next, slowly fading into the surroundings around me, always there, but not really necessary. Only acknowledged when I do something wrong rather than the other hundred things I do right.

I wish I would have kept to myself, phoned my husband and pretended to care that he had been called away for a last minute work emergency on our tenth wedding anniversary getaway when all I really felt was indifference. Then I could have wandered down the cobblestone streets slightly buzzed but completely content. I would have gone up to our hotel room, snuggled with a blanket on the balcony under a Tuscan sky with my e-reader. I'd have devoured those books I've come to love—the ones that have helped me reawaken my sexuality. The books that have made me realize it's okay to want more out of my sex life, to want my husband to push the envelope with me. Experiment with me. Demand more of me.

But I didn't.

I looked up and into eyes the color of dark chocolate, sinful and delicious. Irresistible. Instant attraction sparked with a subtle nod of his head and a bite of my lower lip. I met him stare for stare, a smirk ghosting his mouth as his eyes scraped across my features – lips, cleavage, wedding ring on my finger – before coming back to meet mine. We continued to stare at each other, his eyes darkening with desire and tongue darting out to wet his lips. I suddenly became uncomfortable with the blatant proposition his eyes offered – and averted my gaze. And even then, I could still feel his eyes on me, the hair on my arms standing on end from the feeling of being watched, studied, and scrutinized.

From being desired.

I should have refused the drink the bartender slid in front of me with a murmured, "Compliments of *il signore*." I should have let it sit there untouched instead of drinking most of it, only to stare at remnants and the melting ice cubes.

I should have.

I wish I had.

But I didn't.

My body shivers from a potent cocktail of fear mixed with traitorous pleasure. The heightened sensation shocks my mind back to the present. To the here and now. To the gloved hand sliding a fingertip between my breasts, to the ragged breathing of the man I can't see, to the unknown rifling through me.

And the deep-seated ache to be owned.

I should have never looked up.

His fingers slide between my spread legs and push apart my lips, wet and swollen, a result of everything he's done to me thus far.

Resistance is long gone.

Shame has been obliterated.

Fear remains, a cold and callous presence. But so does the unexpected desire that barrels through my body like a freight train.

I cry out at the feeling of two leather-gloved fingers as they push their way into me, the texture of the material an oddly pleasurable feeling. I'm so raw, so over-sensitized, so used, that I don't think I can take much more. I try to close my legs and my mind is so consumed and overwhelmed that I forget, *I can't*. Forget about the unforgiving restraints holding my ankles apart.

My body begins to writhe, its need to sate the burning ache a sharp contrast to the warring emotions in my psyche. My only focus is on the slow slide in of his fingers and the pressure and friction against nerves unexpectedly reawakened. The tortuous withdrawal of leather not wet enough tugging softly on the most tender of flesh, causing a different but equally arousing sensation.

I try to fight it.

At least I tell myself I do.

I try to understand how this is possible. How an orgasm can rip me apart right now—again—when fear still holds my breath captive.

I should have never accepted the drink, never

looked up to acknowledge him with a subtle nod of my head.

My body vibrates as the swell of white-hot heat sears through me, taking nerve endings hostage and overwhelming all thoughts.

I shouldn't have looked up.

No.

I should've let his silent proposition fall by the wayside.

The question is, why am I glad that I did?

Chapter 2

Last night

THE WEDGE OF my sandal falls in the cracks of the cobblestones causing me to stumble. I laugh aloud at how ridiculous I must look to the patrons of the little bistro bar I've just left. Lonely, pathetic woman getting drunk while on vacation by herself. Using a few drinks to ease the sting of being chosen second best to work once again. I shrug away the true but unwelcome thoughts as a sharp pang of anger hits me because … they're right.

And the sad thing is that if Anderson were here, I'd probably feel even more alone than I do now. We'd have sat at the bar and gotten buzzed without saying much to one another, both of our minds on the numerous things we needed to do when we got back home. We'd have thought about things that could wait a few more days instead of focusing on the whole reason we took this trip: to reconnect, to reprioritize, to recommit.

So I'd have sulked in the silence we've grown accustomed to while thinking of what-could-have-beens and when exactly we stopped communicating. Eventually he'd have asked me what was wrong, to which I'd have replied the over-generalized, and my term of choice as of late, *fine*. He'd have looked toward my wrist to see if I was fiddling with the bracelet I wear and never take off—the surefire way for him to know I'm bluffing. Then depending on if I was or wasn't, either an argument would've ensued where I'd be told to lighten up some or we'd go back to the hotel room where we would have some underwhelming sex.

The *same* sex we've been having for the last ten of our fifteen years together.

Uncreative.

Routine.

Predictable.

And because we would've been drinking, my body wouldn't be able to concentrate on the task at hand—an orgasm. The miraculous aligning of stars that must occur to reach my release would've been unattainable. I'd just have lain there and moaned at all the right times with his alcohol laced breath panting in my face. I'd have taken his drunken, less than pleasurable love-making, and recall times when we couldn't wait to ravish each other. The times we used to push limits that were considered taboo to this preacher's daughter, and how he'd drawn this sexually modest girl from her bubble and dared her to try new things.

I snort out a laugh. How times have changed and roles have reversed. I'd give anything to try something new, push boundaries, explore the sexuality I've now found and accepted with age. Open us up to new experiences, new toys, and redefine new limits.

Jesus. It's sad that I'll give myself a stronger climax using my fingers to get myself off tonight than if Anderson were here. All I have to do is think of things I want to try, imagine him doing them to me, and coming is not a problem. The problem is I can't spend the rest of my life deriving satisfaction from thoughts alone, but every time I've attempted to bring up how to spice up our sex life, he's shut down the topic instantly. *"We're not in our twenties, our sex life is great, why change things?"* the standard given response.

Does he not see how unhappy I am? How I need more sexually? My mind shifts to our last conversation on the topic. The one that happened a couple of months ago when he found the box of toys I had hidden in the bottom of my closet—the items I've secretly bought and kept with the hopes of one day showing and asking him to use on me. I recall how he walked up with the lid off and looked at me, brows furrowed and grimace of disgust on his lips. His disbelief stemming from the fact that I'd bought all of it without consulting him. I can still hear the refusal on his lips, the disconnect in his tone believing that I don't think he's not enough for me anymore, when that's not the case at all.

My dissatisfaction has nothing to do with him not being enough, and everything to do with me coming into my own. Being a woman who's hit her sexual prime and finally after ten years has the confidence and security to ask for what I want.

Nothing crazy, just ... *more*: restraints, domination, anal play, adding a little pain to enhance the pleasure. Something. *Anything.* A slow ache coils in my lower belly as I imagine how hard I'd come if Anderson would use any combination of them on me.

God, I'm pathetic, but … it's not too much to ask, *is it*?

I laugh again—the hollow sound of it ringing more pathetic than cheerful as I ponder if I'm losing it, talking to myself about the experimental, boundary pushing sex I'm never going to have with Anderson.

"Yep, you're losing it all right, Lil." My voice slurs some and sounds odd—off—as it hits my ears. I focus on placing my hand along the building beside me for support because I suddenly feel drunker than I should. And I wonder how sad it is that everything seems so much easier with him being called away to work.

The memories flash through my mind of our first five years together. We used to be fun, adventuresome, imaginative. We'd make sure no surface was left unchristened and orgasms were mutual. I smile forlornly, thinking of when I used to give him spontaneous blow jobs while he drove us home or how his hand would wander underneath my skirt at a restaurant and test if I was wet enough. And if I wasn't, he'd order desert and sit there, draw out the meal, his fingers idly playing between the juncture of my thighs.

I stop for a moment and hold a hand to my stomach when it growls, the realization hitting that I forgot to eat dinner. That must be why I'm so buzzed from only a couple of drinks. I think of the text Anderson had sent me earlier in the day. The one saying my anniversary surprise would arrive in a few hours. To trust him. To remember when.

And then I remember the box of chocolate covered strawberries the bellhop delivered to my room right as I was leaving. How I set the box down with the card unopened because I knew the gift was Anderson's way of softening the blow of his absence. His usual throwback gift to remind me of those earlier, carefree times of ours, since we can't seem to have any for the life of us these days. His way of saying hold-on, things will get better soon. To trust him that we'll get back to where we were before.

But how can they get better if he won't let me explain how we can fix them?

I shake my head at his *remember when*: the night we ate chocolate covered strawberries and drank champagne. Our college days when we were broke so we indulged at his sister's art exhibit before we snuck out and had sex on the venue's rooftop. We'd fucked carelessly, hands over each other's mouths as we tried to be quiet, the thrill of being caught an adrenaline rush all in itself.

When I saw the strawberries I wasn't reminded of what was, but rather was forced to see what no longer is. How life happened. Kids. Corporate promotions and stressful jobs. Time never idle and exhaustion being the new norm.

The tears burn their way up the back of my throat and sting my eyes as my thumb reaches over and rubs my wedding ring. I love him. I really do. He's been mine since our senior year in high school. He's an incredible father to our boys, a hard worker, and treats me incredibly, but I sometimes wonder if this is all there really is for us.

We've fallen in a rut. Life has gotten in the way. Sapped the passion and recklessness. And this trip was our way to reconnect, our way to rekindle everything we once felt and find the "us" we know is there but has been snuffed out by the daily grind.

I sigh, suddenly feeling sad as I realize that I miss him. That I even miss his no surprises, always on cue missionary sex. The twice a week scheduled mattress time that in no way rivals the spontaneous, push you up against the door, rip your clothes off, carnal fucking within the pages of my books. God, what I'd give for Anderson to bend me over, pull my hair back, and make me take what he gives me.

I sigh. I must really be drunk. I would never admit this to myself otherwise, because once you admit truths, you have to face them. And right now, the only thing I want to face is a certain hot alpha racecar driver on my Kindle. A stereotypical example of the book boyfriends Anderson now teases me about, tells me I'd rather sleep with them than him.

The reality is, *he's right*. The characters on the pages don't fall in ruts or have sex that's lackluster. They are fiery and passionate and so easy to get lost in.

"*Here I come*," I mutter—or maybe I think it—I'm not sure, but I do know that I giggle at the double entendre. And then I have to stop a second to combat a wave of dizziness. I begin to walk again, but my head's so fuzzy I can't concentrate on anything other than the sound of my uncoordinated footsteps echoing off the cobblestones.

I reach a small row of alleys, one of which leads to my hotel, but I'm having trouble focusing on them long enough to decide which one to take. Another wave of dizziness assaults me, and I press both hands against the wall to steady myself. I drop my head down and try to breathe in as the blackness seeps into the edges of my vision.

"*Bellisima*?" The deep timbre of the accented voice startles me. I try to process the word, struggle to focus on why my brain tells my head to turn and look toward it, but my muscles don't react. I hear some incoherent sounds and can't comprehend why they sound like they're coming from me.

I'm disoriented but I most definitely feel the hands that slide around my waist, know I'm being tugged back against the solid steel of a man. There is nothing in my body functioning enough that tells me to fight his hold. My sluggish brain tries to process resistance but fires unsuccessfully. Peppermint mixed with an earthy cologne infiltrates my nose, scars my senses.

I can't make sense of anything, except for the peppermint—the scent of my childhood. Of warmth and home and fires in the fireplace during the holidays.

And then he speaks again.

Candy canes and the idea of comfort vanish.

His simple words change my world forever.

"No one has claimed you yet, no?" he says, pausing as a hand covers my mouth to prevent the scream I tell myself to emit but never really sounds. "*Bene*. You are mine, then."

A shiver of terror ricochets through me and takes ownership of my every nerve. It permeates through the miasmic haze closing in on my consciousness, but it's too late.

Darkness wins the battle.
Consumes me.
My world slips away.

Chapter 3

I HEAR MY breath first.

Not the beat of my heart.

Just the ragged, stuttered rasp as I breathe in and then the uncertainty in it as I exhale.

My heart is quiet. Frozen with fear. Silenced by the unknown.

I'm concentrating, trying so hard to not move—to pretend to be asleep so that whoever did this to me still thinks I still am. I'm so focused on not moving that for a moment I don't register the pressure on my eyes, don't realize I'm blindfolded.

My thoughts scatter.

The only one I can grab onto is about the drink from the bar. The one the brown-eyed man bought for me. Then blacking out in the alley. The inability to think, to grasp complete thoughts adds bewilderment on top of confusion .

My head is still in a state of haze, but it recognizes one thing and one thing only—fear. Empty, panicked shouts ricochet around in my brain but cannot escape, cannot manifest themselves into a scream.

The bed beneath me is luxuriously comfortable. The thought flashes through my head, and I struggle to comprehend why in the midst of my chaotic emotions my mind picks to think about this, to concentrate on this. But I cling to the thought, hold onto something tangible to fixate on rather than the unknown that surrounds me.

My mouth is dry and my jaw feels sore, tired. I struggle and break through the fog momentarily, then frantically dive back under when thoughts connect, synapses fire, and realization hits. Something is lodged between my front teeth. I'm bound and gagged. Fear mixes with anxiety as my mind emerges from the haze. I immediately move my hands to remove it and realize I can't. My arms are stretched out at my sides and restrained at my wrists, as are my legs.

A gentle strain on them from an unforgiving hold.

My heart thaws only to be overtaken by a new sensation.

Terror.

Unfettered panic begins to reign. Body wracking tremors attack my limbs as I begin to struggle, fear owning me, the need to escape overwhelming me. I try to yell for help but all that comes out is a muffled sound as I thrash my head back and forth. I buck and writhe my body, my head still groggy but my body on high alert, consumed with the unknown and the never-ending darkness I see. I struggle to breathe, to think, but all I can focus on is that I've been kidnapped. I've been taken against my will, and I've watched enough true crime television shows to know what happens to women in situations like this.

I struggle again, yanking against the restraints with all my might. The only results I have to show for my efforts are aching joints and muscles screaming just as loud as the despair in my soul.

Nothing gives.

Nothing gives except for my first strands of hope.

A tear leaks out. I wait for the feel of it sliding down my cheek, but it doesn't because it's absorbed immediately by the cloth covering my eyes. I attempt to swallow and gag on the bile wanting to escape, just like I do. I try to calm myself down, flee the mind-numbing fear that takes hold but I can't. Not only have I been taken and held against my will, but so has my most important sense: my sight.

No one knows I'm here, wherever here is. Not a single soul.

Oh fuck!

It hits me—the direness of the situation and slams into me head-on.

The tears flow uncontrollably now, my body jarring from the vigor of my sobs. Hopelessness sets in momentarily. And then I get pissed. Pissed at myself for giving up when nothing's happened yet. I try to calm down, attempt to tell myself there is a rational explanation for all of this. That this is all a mistake, a misunderstanding.

And then the hysteria bubbles up and its laughter catches in my throat as I realize how dumb that sounds. A misunderstanding? My laughter ceases immediately, my mind unable to pick one thing and focus on it.

And then I do.

The boys.

Oh god. *My boys.* Will I ever see them again? Will I ever hear their laughs and smell the scent of dirt against their skin after a T-ball game? Hear their deep belly laughs? Feel their pudgy hands on my cheeks as they tell me they love me?

My breath comes faster. Hard, sharp draws of air as I try to shove the sheer panic down, try to lock it up so I don't draw those beautiful little souls into the abyss of darkness that I'm in.

Despair is overtaken by resolve and the will to fight—to survive whatever it is that is going to happen to me—rides shotgun right along with it. I buck and struggle against my restraints, the cool sheets on the bed beneath me growing warm with my defiance. Nothing budges. Absolutely nothing. My head hurts and stomach churns. Defeat settles over me as I try to calm myself, gather my wits, and figure out what to do next.

And then I hear a sound.

The creak of the floor as if someone is shifting their weight and I freeze; my breath, my heart, my body stops, but my mind races.

The floor warns of movement again, and I force a swallow down my throat. The fear is still there running rampant, but it's the anticipation now that kills me. The need to know who is there, what he's doing, what he's planning on doing to me. So many scenarios flicker and flash and none of them are welcome.

I flinch violently when I feel the warmth of his breath against my cheek and smell the peppermint again. He's close, inches from me, and my skin breaks out in goose bumps, the chill coming from the inside. I strain to listen and without my sight I have nothing to rely on, which causes every single one of my senses to be amplified. And it's this hypersensitivity that allows me to feel the chills race across my flesh, that allows me to realize what I couldn't before in my fear-induced panic.

I'm naked.

Completely naked except for my blindfold, my gag, and my restraints.

I try to hold back the sob as his breath continues to heat my cheek, and I attempt to get a handle on the terror, but I fail miserably. I sob as I think about the possibilities of what might happen next. Then my thoughts shift to my kids. Then Anderson. Oh my God. Oh my God.

His text from earlier flickers briefly then fades.

Trust me.

I know he meant trust him to get our marriage back on track, fix things between us. I know they have no relevance to the here and now, but for some reason I cling to those words. Hold on to them to keep a tight grasp on my sanity.

Get a grip, Lilly. Pull it together. I tell myself over and over as my blindfold is so damp with tears the fabric begins to cry itself. I focus on the peppermint smell, trying to pull up the comforting memories from the depths of my mind. The recollections an endless reel of images to lose myself in.

I gasp and become paralyzed, my memories cruelly snagged away as a finger trails over my collarbone.

It moves purposefully from one end to the other and then slowly, tortuously back to its starting point. He makes no sound, no other movement, just a fingertip pressed to my skin so all that rages in my ears is my shuddered breaths mingled with my pulse.

Time passes. Seconds? Minutes? I'm unsure because it feels like an eternity sitting in this suspended state of the unknown.

He sighs into the room and it hangs there like a hand waiting to smother me.

"*Bellisima, vuoi essere il mio amante*?" His murmured voice hits my ears, a deception to my senses, because even though I don't understand him, I know it's sexual in content. I know his voice sounds seductive, but it's what he's going to do to me that stops any part of my body from reacting.

"Don't be scared, sweet bella. I won't hurt you." He laughs, rich and amused, and I'm confused, trying to draw into myself and away from him because I know that laugh is a ruse to trust him. To not fight him when I'm sure he'll violate my body. Scar my mind. Steal my soul. His laughter stops when I whimper.

"You think I lie? You think that I want to hurt this beautiful body of yours?" His voice is firmer now with a touch of anger, a result of my disbelief. The bed shifts as he gets off it, and behind my blindfold my eyes move as if I'm watching. My ears strain to track which direction he is going. "This body is mine. *Your body is mine*. I do not hurt what is mine."

I start trembling again. My toes curl and then relax, the only movement I voluntarily make under his quiet scrutiny I can't see but can feel. Processing his words is just too much—everything too much—because all I can focus on is being at this man's mercy.

His slave.

His next whim.

"I will give your body pleasure—take the pleasure you give me willingly—"

Like hell I'll give him anything of me. "*Fuck you.*" The garbled sound is out of my mouth before I can think, and I realize my mistake a second too late.

Spikes of pain light across my right breast, pin pricks that sting causing my nipples to harden instantly. My breath hitches and I arch my back in reflex to the bites into my flesh, my only reaction to combat the unexpected pain.

And I start thrashing my head from side to side as the contradiction of his words and actions hit me. He's not going to hurt me? Then what the hell was that? My body vibrates with trepid anticipation because the silence is killing me. I want him to talk again. If he talks then maybe I won't be obsessively focused on the silence, on the creaks of the floor, on waiting for the next blow to strike.

His hand presses on my neck, covering the entirety of it, and forces my chin up. My mind races. My body freezes. His undetected approach reaffirms my unchallenged vulnerability. Silence screams between us, our only connection his hand pressed against my throat. My lips shock apart when I feel the heat of his breath against my cheek. And yet he doesn't move, doesn't speak, just remains there, reminding me of his constant presence.

An unknown amount of time stretches. When he

finally speaks, there is an unprovoked bite in his tone. "Do not fucking question me. Do not talk back. Is that understood?" I can't find my voice to answer because I'm focusing so hard on trying to find the breath that he's robbed from me. "Is that understood?" I nod my head as best as I can with his hand still pressed there. "I will fuck you as I see fit. I will use you, own you, make you mine." I feel his tongue slide down the line of my jaw to the lobe of my ear, and I fight the shudder of revulsion that riots within. His lips brush against my skin. "And when I've taken everything I want from you, I will let you go."

My head startles at his last words. "*What*?" The word falls from my mouth but all I hear is an incoherent mess of sound. He's going to let me go? The question is in what condition will I be left when he's done with me? It doesn't matter. *I can do this.* I can survive this—anything—if it means I get to go home to my boys.

My moment of skeptical joy is halted when his finger begins a slow descent over my collarbone. This time he stops when it hits my midline and starts to move down between my breasts. My body shivers at the feeling—at the coarse tug of my skin against his finger, and I realize he is wearing gloves. Leather gloves, I think. The material pulls on my skin, an odd contrast to the gentle nature of the touch causing chills to dance and disquiet to own my every fiber.

He stops at my lower abdomen, and although he leaves his finger there, the floorboards broadcast his methodical movements. I frantically track the sounds as he walks around the perimeter of my bed, my prison.

My chest deflates and body freezes—fear firing anew despite his words promising relief. I feel the bed dip near the end by my feet and the anticipation of what is going to happen is almost as numbing as the fear that is now a constant.

His finger never moves, but I can feel it shake, the bed sway, as he adjusts his positioning, and it's ridiculous because I can't see him, but I swear I can feel his eyes scraping over every inch of me. Observing. Assessing.

I force a swallow over the fear that chokes me and mentally prepare myself for what's coming next. The pain, the brutality, the loss of my consent. I try to control my trembling because I have to assume he likes the fight—is turned on by it—so if I don't give it to him, will this be over that much quicker? Will he discard me and move on to someone who gives him what he wants? Because let's face it, only sick fucks get off on shit like this, and if I don't give it to him, won't he want someone who will?

I garble a cry at the unexpected, my body and mind shocking to the present when the wet warmth of his tongue traces the seam between my thighs. I try to snap my thoughts in line, but his unpredicted action bewilders me long enough that I don't even think to fight him. And because my body is still and my senses attuned, I can feel the softness of his tongue, the languorous, heat-inducing trail it blazes up to my clit, circling over it not just once, but twice, before sliding back down and deftly parting my folds down to my opening.

My breathing shallows, my teeth bite down on

the gag, and I attempt to comprehend, assess, come to terms with what I'm feeling. How I can be scared boneless and yet still have that slow burning ache unfurling in my lower belly. I tell myself I'm crazy—that my mind is playing games on me, my subconscious shutting down so I can compartmentalize everything—but I know I'm kidding myself. I can't even concentrate long enough to sell myself my own lies because it's impossible to ignore, impossible to deny the traitorous warmth that spreads through my core and simmers there. Amidst the haze of desire that assaults me, my rationale tries one more attempt—one last ditch effort, because there is no way in hell I should even be remotely turned on by his touch on my skin, his tongue delving into me.

I shouldn't.

But I am.

I adjust my hips some, tell myself it's not real, but the ache doesn't dissipate with movement. And in response to my squirming, his finger leaves my skin for the first time but is back instantly, this time in a different place. Hands grip my inner thighs and pin them immobile. I'm still gasping in the air from the sudden, bruising hold he has on my legs when his tongue plunges into me.

My cry is involuntary. The buck of my hips and arch of my back in response isn't even a coherent thought but rather a reflex. I fight to ignore the blissful warmth between my thighs, rationalize that it's my body's natural reaction, that I won't succumb to his persuasion of pleasure.

Pleasure that's unwelcome.

Pleasure that is still pleasure.

His tongue slips in, wetting me, opening me up, manipulating me. My nerves ride a disloyal roller coaster as he plunges in, circles around, and then withdraws to slide up, circling my clit, sucking on it, igniting it, before moving back down and licking back into me.

The first moan that falls from my mouth startles me. My logic attempts to validate why my body reacts this way when I should be locked like a vice … but I can't focus on anything because his tongue just keeps moving: up, down, in, out, around and around. A tantalizing assault that leaves my head reeling and my body humming.

My muscles tighten as his fingers dig deeper and his tongue laves more fervently. I can hear his panted breath. It disrupts the silence of the room, but the other sound I hear is even more disturbing: my own stifled moans as I try to fight the sensation swelling through me. Time lapses and warmth spreads, nerves ignite, and then my body detonates, splintering into a million pieces of pleasure.

I have no choice but to succumb to the tidal wave that hits and then drowns me momentarily. I can't close my legs or relax my body as I normally would, so for some reason the exposure makes my orgasm seem more intense, more explosive.

More traumatic—emotionally and physically.

His hands hold me—my muscles still spasming against his possessive fingers—when I feel his lips press against my inner thigh. They curve into a smile against my sensitized flesh like a familiar lover would, and the contradiction hits me—the tenderness displayed in a situation so contrary—makes it that much harder to process what just happened. What I just succumbed to and derived pleasure from.

Oh my God. Oh my God.

What is wrong with me? How can I find pleasure from this man who is holding me against my will? What kind of sick, fucked up person am I? How can I even remotely be turned on?

The bile rises. I try to fight it, try to swallow it down. My head becomes light and my breath shallow as my body becomes starved for the air it needs. I begin gagging, coughing violently, trying to revolt against the object in my mouth. I can't dislodge it. I yank against my restraints, buck my body as I seek my next breath.

In an instant his hands are at my head. I feel them tug and manipulate something. I focus on the peppermint again, use it to calm myself, but with the blitzkrieg of sensations and emotions hitting me, my connection to the scent is losing its effectiveness. My head dizzies as his mouth brushes up against my ear. "Bella, Bella, Bella," he soothes with the deep timbre of his voice. "Calmare la mia bella. Breathe slowly," he commands as I feel his body against mine, his hands at the corners of my mouth. "Calm down."

Panic continues its smothering grip on my reality, and I shake my head back and forth trying to shove the gag from my mouth with my tongue. He holds my jaw firm, his heated breath against my hair. "Do not scream. I will remove this, but if you scream, I will put a bigger one in and then there's no telling how much air you'll get with your next panic attack. *Capisci?* Understood?"

My breath rattles in my throat as I try to gulp down air I still can't draw. My thoughts elevating from the depths of despair in which they've fallen into momentarily at the chance to yell for help, but I forget them as my consciousness starts to fade.

"Say it goddamn it!"

His voice jars me from the darkness edging my mind, and I try to nod my head in response, but his fingers holding my jaw prevent the action. I know he wants me to say the words aloud, my voice affirming his position of control.

"Yes." I garble.

The gag is removed immediately. I suck in air like a drowning man breaking the surface. My head dizzies again, but this time from the returning oxygen. I choke on the air as I suck it in, in greedy bouts. My mind feels like it can think relatively clearly for the first time since I've awakened into this nightmare.

He backs away to give me some space, but I can still feel his presence. Shouting at the top of my lungs is my first thought, but I can't see anything. Is he pointing a gun at me? Does he have a knife? Do I risk the chance since I'm literally and figuratively blind?

I make a conscious decision not to scream. To choose to comply. And it seems stupid but everything else about this situation is out of my control so I grab onto the one option that he provides me.

Besides, I'm so thankful to breathe again that I don't want to risk having the gag put back in my mouth. I dart my tongue out to lick my dry, chapped lips and work my jaw back and forth, my ears popping from the motion. "*Why?*" I croak the word out in a broken rasp. It's all I allow myself to say, fear of repercussions holding the rest of my accusations hostage.

His chuckle is soft, but I can hear the rumble in his chest and my goose bumps return. "Oh, my beautiful Lilly," he says causing my heart to thunder and my world to stop. My *name* rolls over his accented tongue as if he's fucking it, and it's an odd mix of derision and the unexpected that courses through me.

I remind myself that I've been unconscious for some time; he's had time to rifle through my purse and find out things about me such as my name. But that means he's also seen pictures of Anderson, my family, *my boys*.

And the shame immediately hits me. My husband knows my body better than anyone, so how can this person I just met and who is holding me against my will bring me to orgasm so quickly? I squeeze my eyes tight, the whole premise hard to swallow. I exhale a deep sigh as I clench and unclench my fists for circulation, giving myself a moment to control the civil war of emotions raging within. My moment of peace—if you can actually call it that—is short lived because he begins speaking again.

"*Mia bella Lilly* ..." his finger presses down on the top of my right foot and trails a slow path up my shin much the same way he did over my collarbone earlier. It's as if he wants every part of my body aware of his presence—as if it's not already. "Because sometimes a person knows just what another might need even if they never utter the words. Your eyes speak truths you don't. You are gorgeous, no? This body of yours tempts me, taunts me..." he continues the ascent of his finger up my thigh at a lethargic pace "...begs me to take it. And look," he says as he slides his fingertip softly between my thighs. I tense immediately as he rubs his fingers up and back through my wetness before withdrawing, the cool air of the room a sharp contrast against my heated flesh.

My exhale startles out of me when his fingertip rubs across my lower lip. "What are—"

"You want me just as bad," he says into my ear as he coats my lips with my own arousal. "You are drenched," he murmurs as the bed dips beside me, and I try to move my head from his demonstration of my body's blatant betrayal. He holds my jaw still, leaning in so I can feel his breath feather across my lips.

My mind races. Thoughts, threats, prayers combine into a potent combination of resolve.

"*Why you?*" he murmurs. I feel his lips brush against mine, and I squirm from the touch.

Come closer, I silently dare him as I clench my fists. *Come closer and I'll bite your tongue if you try to kiss me, you fucker*.

"Ahhhh," he sighs, tapping a finger against my curled hands. "The fighter in you returns, no? Why fight what deep down you know you want? I doubt your husband will ever fuck you like I will. I doubt he takes the time to make your body ache so much it hurts."

His finger slides down the column of my throat before he presses his hand there. My pulse pounds against the pads of his fingers, a physical manifestation of the emotions rioting within me. His grip tightens as he leans in and uses his tongue to trace the outline of my trembling lips. When he finishes, he pulls away, but

I can still feel him there, his presence so formidable he might as well be touching me.

"Does he know how turned on you are by being at my mercy? How your body craves to be violated, dominated, fucked hard, used at my every whim?" He chuckles low and deep. "I doubt he's fucked every inch of your body like I will."

My muscles tense, his threat causing my breath to catch in my throat, my mind visiting places I don't want it to. Images flash of wants and desires too taboo in Anderson's eyes, and I chastise myself for being turned on by this man's words.

By my captor's words.

Anger fills me and begins to consume my every fiber, but the most confusing part of it all is whom the anger is directed at. It's not at him—no, it's at me. Because as hard as it is to hear the words and the truths they cause, in the end, he's right. My body trembles with the acknowledgement because as much as I deny it, this is what I've wanted from Anderson.

Dirty talk.

Provocation and domination.

Curiousity edged with a nervous excitement as we push limits.

I try to shut down my mind, attempt to ignore my body and recall the reserved woman I am, the one I used to be—because hell if I know who this woman is that wants this stranger to fuck her how he's promising—and gain back an ounce of the fight and determination that I need right now. I shove the unwanted thoughts out, try to clear my head and it takes me a moment but I find it. At least my words say that I have, my mind on the other hand is still left to be convinced.

"Go to hell," I grate out between my gritted teeth.

That laugh again. Amusement mingled with superiority rings through the room. "Bella, by the time I'm done with you, you'll be begging me to fuck you again. You'll beg to suck my cock, to fuck your mouth. You'll yearn to please me, crave my touch. You'll cry when I leave you to go back to your everyday life."

His words cause an intense, unfathomable ache to unfurl in my core. Blood swells the tender flesh there, and even though I have this man in front of me holding me against my will, the oddest feeling comes over me. *I believe him when he says he doesn't want to hurt me.* I have no basis for this belief, just my gut instinct, but in some fucked up sense I trust him.

Now what does that say about me?

I divert my thoughts elsewhere. I don't have the wherewithal to look closer at myself, a surefire way to fuck my head up even further. But all I can think is that this man captured me. He captured me and then brought me pleasure by licking me to orgasm. He hasn't even penetrated me yet. He could have thrust into me with complete disregard to my readiness or my pleasure, as I assumed would've happened, and gotten off.

But he didn't.

He hasn't used me and tossed me aside how I'd have expected. I shiver as the air conditioner kicks off, and I strain to hear the sounds of life outside of the room. A car honks in the distance but not a single sound in the room. My thoughts run wild again, my attention so schizophrenic that I welcome their distraction. I hold onto that—the disorder, the confusion—so that I can lose focus, lose myself, in order to hold onto the hope.

And then the pain hits.

Chapter 4

PAIN SEARS.

Fire ignites against my flesh.

I scream out, my body jerking, back arching, and nipples tightening, as something singes my chest spot after spot. My mind races—a flash of coherency between each bite of pain—and focuses solely on where I think the next place will be.

Hot wax.

My skin chills but then burns.

Drip.

"Pain can bring pleasure, mia bella," he murmurs as another drop falls, and I hiss to combat the hurt. "Pain can make your nerves sensitive."

Drip.

"Can make your body overcompensate in other ways."

Drip.

I struggle to pull myself from the hypnotic fixation on where it will drop next. I want to scream at him to stop. Want to ask him how he can say no pain and then he does this. Why he lied.

My mind finally forms the words, my tongue readies to say them when they are knocked clear off my lips.

His mouth closes over my nipple. The unexpected move—the warm, wet feeling of him adding tantalization to my torment—has my back bowing and a strangled sigh falling from my lips. I relax some, relieved the drips of wax may be on hiatus, my mind focused for so long on the pain that the pleasure is unexpectedly heightened. The movement of his tongue, the contrast of sucking hard and then laving softly, mainlines an electric current to my core that I don't have an ounce of strength to fight.

And the difference this time is that his body is against mine, pressing me into the softness of the mattress beneath us. The taut muscles of his abdomen rub between the juncture of my thighs when he moves up my body so his mouth can pleasure my right breast. His hand squeezes my other one, fingers pinching, manipulating, and then a pressure edging on pain closes around my nipple.

My mind is yanked cruelly from concentrating on his mouth, my breath hissing in, my head angling up as if I would be able to see what he's doing. The sting is slight, but combined with the wax and his mouth, every inch of my body hums and rides on a high alert. His teeth nip and tug again before he releases my tightened bud, and then I feel matching pain there as well.

He pulls justly on whatever connects the two nipple clamps.

My breath catches in my throat.

Drip.

I cry out at the unexpected sensation when I thought it was over.

His chuckle resonates in the room, scarring its way into my memory just as the wax singes my flesh. His body lifts, my own easing up from the mattress without his weight on me. The bed sways and then stills.

And then nothing.

The silence hits again, smothers my mind and heightens my anticipatory fear. The floorboards announce his movement and something clatters onto the floor

And I wait.

The ice cold chill hits my skin, a gasped "ahhh" falling from my mouth.

"Silence," he commands. And I fight the urge to gasp when he rubs the ice cube around my nipple. It hardens to the point of pain and the sensation mixed with the clamping causes a bewildering surge of arousal. He continues his tantalizing torture of the cubes around my breasts, up to the hollow of my throat and then back down.

He circles my navel and then lets it rest in the hollow of my belly button. The chill of the cube sitting idly begins to burn subtly, causing me to squirm.

"Ah, bella Lilly," he murmurs, and I can hear the smile I remember from my glance at the bar in his voice. "Do not move. Do not let the water spill over. Not one drop. The only other thing allowed to be wet is this pussy of yours." His fingers are on my opening, spreading my sex apart. I tense at the feeling—invading fingers on my most intimate parts—and I can feel the growing drop of water on my stomach fall over the dip of my navel and run down my stomach.

"Ah, you are dripping for me, no? You like fire and ice?"

My body trembles as he slips two fingers in me and bends them before pulling them slowly back out. My eyes roll back and a moan comes from deep within as he continues his assault, plunging into me and then curving to hit my g-spot perfectly on their way out. He draws sensations from me that are so intense, so powerful, that there is no way I can suppress them. I begin to writhe, begin to lift my hips for him, grant him access as my body begs him to sate the need he's created.

"If it spills, you'll be punished," he warns as his fingers withdraw completely causing me to suddenly feel empty and dangling on the brink of release. "… You will make me go back on my word not to hurt you." He tsks. "I don't like to be forced to break promises."

My mind registers his forewarning, but my body couldn't care less when I feel something push into me. The water on my stomach, the heeded advice—none of it matters because all I can concentrate is the slow insertion of something ice cold, inch by thick inch into me. Chills race over my flesh. They are so severe I can feel the hardened wax pull from my skin as he begins to slowly pull the frozen object back out. I angle my hips, try to relieve the extremity of the temperature, when whatever is within me hits the soft nerve-laden spot within. I begin yanking my legs against my restraints. The intensity of the mixture—cold against sensitivity—is almost too much for me to bear.

The room fills with my cry and his chuckle—an odd juxtaposition of sound—as my body fights the sensations resulting from his machinations. His hand stills, the iced wand remains unwelcome but wanted within me, and the only sound in the room is the harsh rasp of our panted breaths.

"You failed." That tsk of his is back, chilling my insides just as the ice does my outsides. "Now, Lilly, you weren't a very good girl." It's all he says but the disappointment in his voice causes a random mix of emotions to swell within. Fear of the punishment, despair over the situation, self-loathing that I was so attuned to what he was doing to me elsewhere that I forgot his singular demand.

I suck in a breath as the bed shifts, unsure of what his definition of punishment is since he said he's not going to hurt me. My mind frantically flickers in its schizophrenic haze, the deafening silence of the room only adding to my unrest. I try not to squirm at the cold between my thighs, but whatever it is, is thawing from my heat. The chilled liquid is seeping out and trickling down my perineum, dripping onto the bed beneath me.

"So many options," he murmurs against my ear, his sudden nearness unexpected and shocks the hell out of me. I hold my breath at the same time his feathers against my cheek. His quiet scrutiny unnerves me, my eyes darting back and forth beneath my blindfold trying to sense his next move.

Trying to predict my punishment.

Punishment. Pain. A small thrill jolts through me right before I realize how seriously disturbing that is.

My core clenches and tightens around the object as I try to rationalize the sick, demented part of me that is aroused by this all. And I'm not allowed to finish the mental chastisement because I feel him climb over my torso. I fall motionless as his muscular thighs press against the sides of my rib cage, his shaft rests between my breasts, thick and heavy.

I fight the forbidden desire that pulses through me at the feeling and try to focus on what he'd said. Punishment. Fear comingles with desire and causes my muscles to constrict with such vigor that I push out the ice within me. A deluge of cold water comes with it, but I fight the gasp because if he's facing me, then he doesn't know. And if he doesn't know then that means that he might not require my penance for that too.

But why do I secretly want him to?

His peppermint breath is back on my lips, his erection squeezed between my breasts as he leans forward. My nipples harden, the swelling increasing the pressure between the clamps. "What I'd give to make you take my cock all the way to the back of your throat. Feel your wet tongue on my dick and suck me dry." Saliva pools in my mouth at his words, my tongue darting out to lick my lips in reflex. His chuckle resonates again, and I can feel his scrotum tighten and release with its sound. "Ah, you want that, no? Well I don't quite trust that your bark is worse than your bite just yet," he says, followed by a quick tug on the clamps.

The release of pressure is sudden but then comes a searing sting as blood flow returns. His weight on my torso stifles my immediate urge to twist and turn as a means to absorb the oddly pleasurable pain tearing through me and manifesting into a deep ache in my lower belly. I moan out and yank my arms and legs against the restraints, trying to relieve the overwhelming sensation somehow, someway.

"You like that, no?" he whispers, his weight shifting so his mouth barely brushes against mine when he speaks. "You see, I need to punish you." He traces his tongue over the seal of my lips. "I need to have my cock buried so fucking deep in that beautiful cunt of yours that when I punish you, it clenches around me. So that you tighten and tease and pull me over the edge with you." I feel the bed shift some, his hips tilt up as he leans back and his fingers enter me hard and fast. Unexpected and invading. The startled cry is muffled on my lips. "I will own this. Your pussy, your orgasm, and every ache, breath, and moan in between."

His fingers thrust in and out momentarily. The room fills with our panting breaths, the slick sound of wet flesh being manipulated, his soft grunts of effort and my pleasured moans as the friction heats up my frozen walls. A liquid warmth starts to spread through my body. The unique combination of my throbbing nipples, the inimitable scent of maleness as his cock thrusts closer to my face, and the claim he takes by fingering me causes my body to seize up and prepare for the climax I fear will rip me apart.

Pray will rip me apart.

"Oh god," I moan out incoherently as my body floats in that suspended state before the eruption of bliss. My head angles back and lips fall lax, my breath hitching and mind stuttering over thoughts as I try to grab and let them go all at once because I'm such a mix of contradictions. The tremors of sensation slowly escalate toward a full blown earthquake when his fingers pull out, and before I even have a chance to respond, the wide crest of his cock is thrust between my parted lips. I'm so shocked from being denied the release my body desperately craves that I can't even react fast enough to deny his thick shaft as it hits the back of my throat and pulls out.

The guttural grown he emits only adds pressure to the denied orgasm weighing heavily between my thighs. I'm turned on, desperate to come, and his musky taste overtaking me only adds frenzy to my fire. And just as quick as he fills my mouth and unintentionally blocks my airway, he withdraws before I can rationalize what he is doing or where my teeth should clamp down.

I gulp in a draw of air as he shifts from the bed once again. His body leaves mine, the slide of his dick across my nipple is oddly arousing, and I want to cry out for him to stop. To come back. To fuck me good and hard because my muscles ache and my need is unsated.

If denying me my orgasm is his punishment, then holy hell, I'll take more wax.

I want to yell at him, insist that he finish me off, but I catch myself before the words tumble out. I realize that such a demand would be giving him exactly what he wants—*exactly what I want*—but under his terms. He has enough of an upper hand in this whole situation and I need to keep something. For what? I'm unsure, but the thought gives me enough gumption to keep my mouth shut despite the ever increasing ache.

His hands on my right wrist snap me from my daze

of thoughts. The building ache is momentarily doused as he works at my restraint. Is he releasing me? My mind processes possible scenarios at a rapid pace as I hold my breath and don't say a word trying to figure how to play this. My joints are relieved of the restraint's unending tension momentarily before his hand is like a vice grip around my wrist. Even if I wanted to try something, my strength would be no match against his.

"Don't even think about it," he says, the quiet warning from somewhere at my side as he forces my arm across my body and to the headboard opposite where it was originally. My hands are now near each other and my legs still spread apart on the bed when he starts working on the opposite wrist. And then I realize what he is doing. He's turning me over.

A thrill shoots through me, followed by trepidation because if I felt vulnerable before, I feel even more so now when he finishes. He has loosened my restraints somehow so I'm able to be on my hands and knees on the bed. In this position, I can feel the cool air of the room against the now heated flesh between my thighs. My breasts hang heavily and the weight of them stretching against my swollen nipples is like a livewire to my core. The blindfold remains in place, and yet I can't help but dart my eyes against the blackness as the floorboards creak toward the end of the bed where my backside is on display.

He groans out in satisfaction and I flinch when the palm of his hand smooths ever so gently over the curve of my ass. "Ah, Lilly. This ass is perfection. I want it pink from your punishment. I want it violated by my fingers. I want it filled while I fuck you long and deep with my cock in that willing pussy of yours." My body trembles and sex moistens from his words, fear and desire a potent combination that is impossible to deny regardless of how hard I'm trying to fight it.

In the silence, my only focus is on the gentle movement of his hand caressing gently over my hips, my inner thighs, over my sex. I moan at the gentleness of his touch as he continuously strokes me, not quite hard enough to add the needed friction to my clit but just enough to have the blood engorging it to that fine edge of being painful.

The strike across my ass takes me by surprise, fooled naively by the gentle nature of his caress. I cry out, back arching, breasts jostling, pussy clenching as the flogger whips little bits of pain into my bare flesh. And as I'm trying to process and absorb the sudden assault—the forewarned punishment—he pushes into me in one slick thrust. My clenched walls give under his invasion but grip his dick so tight that his large crest hits every single attuned nerve within. This time the sound that falls from my lips is a strangled moan mixed with protest.

If I thought he had warmed me up to accept his girth, I was far off base. My vulnerable flesh protests against the stretch with an intense burn.

Pleasure and pain.

I don't think I ever quite understood the magnitude of that phrase until now. Until he starts to move his iron hard erection within me, filling me, stretching me, taking me without asking. And then when he's buried to the hilt, one hand gripping the flesh of my hips, the flogger strikes me again. The difference is this time when my body tenses from the tiny splinters of pain and when my pussy convulses around him, he pulls out so that his broad head drags against my tightened walls. Sparks of pleasure ignite from his unexpected withdrawal.

"Oh god," slips from my lips as my body welcomes the contrast of sensations. And he doesn't stop but rather keeps up a distinct rhythm, his hips slapping against mine while the flogger—what feels like leather with rounded tips—trails slowly over my back. He removes it and my body prepares for the quick flash of pain, and sometimes it lands smartly and other times it caresses in a gentle ruse, tickling my anticipatory flesh beneath it.

I am so focused on the flogger and whether its next movement will bring me pleasure or pain that I don't realize my body vibrates on the cusp of my next orgasm. My back burns with the little licks that have assaulted it, and the muscles within my core ache from clenching so tightly around the thickness of his cock. My head falls forward, my arms weary from what feels like his endless machinations, and my mind is floating in pseudo-reality when my thighs constrict and back rounds.

The orgasm hits me like a runaway freight train: hard, fast, and unrelenting. It's so powerful—so everything—that I try to pull away from him, try to press my hips forward to relieve the depth he's penetrated, but I can't. He grips the flesh on my backside harder, holding me still while he grinds his hips against my ass so just on the off chance he's missed any interior nerves, he's making up for it and then some.

But I can't take any more. The force of the orgasm. The merciless onslaught of sensations barraging my system. "No. Stop. No," I stutter in broken gasps, wanting to crawl away from him. I am able to get one knee forward, and he slips out of me some before his hands are back on my hips yanking me back to him. My yelp only gets louder when his hand wraps around my hair and tugs my head back. His mouth is at my ear, fury laced with a raw carnality that causes my posture to stiffen on the defensive.

"You don't deny me. You take what I give you, bella, and right now, it's me. Hard. Fast," he demands as he slams into me from behind, bottoming out in the best way. In the worst way. I can't process which way because my own climax continues to softly tremor through me, and the dominance in his voice and ownership in his touch spurns the release I just found to reignite. "Until I stop." He reinforces his threat by tightening his grip on my hair as he continues his punishing rhythm, our bodies connecting with a jolt that reverberates through me and then back.

I begin to squirm again as everything increases and draws me toward what feels like the never-ending precipice of ecstasy. My fingers grip the sheets, my toes curl, and breath falters as the sparks of pleasure turn into a full-blown wildfire I can't escape. Burned and bruised by the flames of desire, I have no option but to succumb to the heat pulsing within me. I whimper incoherently and shake my head back and forth as my body begins to collapse under the weight of release. My arms give and my face welcomes the cool sheet pressing against my cheek as he keeps my hips positioned to his liking.

His hips piston continuously for a few more moments, and then I hear the man who seems to always be in control groan out a guttural sound as his cock spasms inside of me. My shoulders push forward into the mattress while he draws out the last of his release. My eyes close, exhaustion overtaking me so that my only comprehension other than the lowering of my hips, is the kiss he presses to the space just above the swell of my ass. An oddly intimate action that normally I'd question, but my body sags and I succumb to the fatigue in my limbs.

I welcome the darkness the blindfold provides and allow myself to block out what his confusing display of tenderness says.

Chapter 5

I CAN HEAR him shuffling around the room. My head is groggy and my stomach is unsettled but my body is boneless, completely and utterly spent. I wait for him to tell me to get up or snap to, but he leaves me be. My back still burns subtly from the punishment he doled out, and the length of my sex is swollen and tender from his continuous usage. My hands are sore from clenching and gripping the sheets, my mind exhausted from trying to rationalize everything in my head. The contrast of feelings, the forced betrayal of my fidelity—everything—has me well beyond emotional overload.

I let the tears flow now, allow the guilt to pull me under as I try and figure out how I'm going to go back to being *me* when this is done. Because without a doubt, I know he's going to let me go. I know he is going to get his fill and discard me. I don't fear that he'll brutalize me and leave me dead on the roadside somewhere, because even though he just put my body through the sexual wringer, he also did so with a misconstrued respect. Never going too far or stepping over what seems to be a predetermined boundary.

And he kissed me gently.

My head spins.

The merry-go-round of confusion is endless.

Since when does a guy abduct a woman, fuck her senseless, and then let her go? If I'm crazy for liking this, then he surpassed my lack of sanity miles ago.

Or orgasms.

The laughter comes now. Hysterical bouts of it that don't belong in this room where consensual is not an option. It bubbles up and over. My mind and body succumb to the desperate sound in its tone, just needing a disruption from the exhaustive, unanswered questions.

And therein lies the problem. Yes he is holding me against my will—fucking me, pleasuring me, punishing me—but my God, I got off on it. What in the hell does that say about me?

I try to turn my mind off, try to allow myself a reprieve because I have no clue how long this is going to last and I'm spent. I just want to sleep, shut down the thoughts and questions I don't want answers to right now. The answers that just might tell me I'm not the person I thought I was. The answers that might unravel the truths I don't want to face.

Time lapses. I lose myself in trying not to think. And then I drift off.

I'm not sure for how long when I'm jolted from my slumbered state. A warm wash cloth runs over my inner thighs and then parts me gently, cautiously, cleaning me up. When he finishes, I'm chilled from the room's air hitting my wet skin, but my attention is easily diverted to the dip of the bed and the feel of one of his hands whispering over my bare backside. I hold my breath immediately, the soft caress unexpected but welcome. A simple gesture of tenderness amidst his never-ending dominance. His hand trails languorously over my hip and then crosses over my back. My skin is still tender to the touch so I try not to flinch when he connects with the welts.

He murmurs something softly under his breath that I don't understand. I tell myself to relax, to just accept his bewildering tenderness, but it's hard to not anticipate another whip of leathered roses against my skin. I withdraw from my thoughts when his lips press against the indent between my shoulder blades, yet another show of affection. I work a swallow over the lump of confusion in my throat as the ache in my core flickers to life.

I try to fight it this time, tell myself that I don't want this, want him or the burn that's beginning to intensify as he laces contradictory kisses to the base of my neck. *But my body has other thoughts.* It betrays me when goose bumps chase in the wake of his tongue as it slowly slides down the length of my spine. I exhale audibly when he reaches the dimples of my lower back and keeps going.

His hands are suddenly on the curve of my ass, pushing me up to my knees so my shoulders press into the mattress and my hips are in the air. He unabashedly grabs the rounded globes and pulls them apart so that his tongue can descend with ease. I suck in a breath, my sex clenching tighter with every inch he covers. We both groan as his tongue licks around the rim. My muscles tense and my breath hitches as my nerve endings set ablaze from the potent combination of his touch and the forbidden notion of it.

I can feel myself becoming wet, can feel the ache intensifying as his tongue skims downward, his fingers firmly kneading my ass. I involuntarily press my hips backwards, a silent plea for more of what I've been told for a lifetime is dirty and wrong. A notion that I don't care about in this moment because the hub of nerve endings he's rimming begs for more—to be experimented and manipulated.

A chair scrapes across the floor on the other side of the room.

What in the hell? I'm jolted from the euphoric edge I can sense my body is climbing toward. My heart races and stops. His hands remain on me, possessive, but his face withdraws from the curve of my body.

"Ahhh, so you want to get a better view Marco, *no*? Your note taking is complete?"

What? My pulse races, pounding a frantic tattoo as it roars through my ears. I want to tell it to shut the hell up so I can hear, so I can figure out who in the fuck is watching me?

Be forced.

Become pleasured.

"No!" I cry the word trying to process why my nipples harden and pussy throbs at the thought of being watched. Of having someone sitting there observing me be taken against my will. Why am I aroused beyond belief at the thought?

My captor chuckles low and mocking, and my every nerve stands on end. His hand fists in my hair, his voice an immediate growl in my ear. He pulls my head back so my neck is exposed and the heat of his body blankets across my back, seeps into any part of me that is chilled from the thought of an onlooker.

"No questions. No denials. Remember the rules?" His tongue traces around the shell of my ear—my surefire erogenous zone—and I fight the urge to shift my hips and relieve the pleasurable pain he's relit. "Behave, mia bella." The heat of his breath hits my ears, the brush of his lips such a stark contrast to the warning he delivers. "I'm going to fuck you. By the time I'm done, you'll beg me to keep going. Then you'll beg me to stop. Regardless, you'll take what I give you—all of it—and you'll enjoy every single fucking moment of it. And Marco is going to watch. Understood?"

The dominance of his words excites me. The notion that someone is going to watch evokes a potent mixture of uncertainty and provocation. I'm so lost in the idea of being taken, being fucked without preamble, along with the feeling of his hardening dick pressed against the crack of my ass that I don't even realize I haven't answered him. His hand closes over my exposed neckline and presses there, forcing my head back and snapping me from my thoughts.

I give an incoherent sound of consent just as I hear Marco move about the room. My ears strain and body attunes to the raw physicality of two men—one I can physically feel, the other I cannot—but both dominating nonetheless. My nipples tighten and skin chills under the scrutiny of eyes I can't see but know are studying my body.

"*Brava, ragazza*," he says to me, hand tightening ever so subtly. "This man handles your fate. He decides what happens next. I told you I won't hurt you, that I'll let you go when I've had my way with you … but if you disappoint him?" He makes a soft tsking sound. I try to swallow at this new development, but the angle of my neck makes it difficult.

A sliver of fear snakes through me.

The hand on my throat slowly slides down over my collarbone as my thoughts race faster than my heart. His hand finds my breasts and palms one of them pressing its weight up against my chest and squeezes.

"If you don't make it worth his while," he chuckles, low and deep. His hand retraces its path back up so that he can insert two fingers into my mouth, forcing me to taste my arousal from earlier. "Well then all bets are off."

I cry out as his free hand slaps my ass hard. The sting reverberates through my body and into my sex with a resonating effect. My hands grip the sheets as his fingers press down against my tongue and hold it still. I feel him move, the bed shifts, the heat of his body leaves mine—skin sliding over skin—and then the mattress moves again as he brings his face close enough so that his nose bumps against mine.

If I thought I felt vulnerable before, it's tenfold now. At least I know the man in front of me doesn't really want to hurt me, but the man at my back? Now he scares me.

His hold on my mouth tightens as he tilts my head up some to what I can assume is the same angle as his. "I'm going to kiss you now. I'm going to see if this mouth of yours tastes just as sweet as your pussy does. You will not bite me. You will kiss me back." He leans forward and presses a pseudo kiss to my lips, slightly hindered by the placement of his fingers. His breath feathers over my lips as he pulls back. "And then I'm going to prepare you for what you want but refuse to admit." He removes his fingers ever so slowly, drawing them down so my bottom lip pulls down with their descent. When my mouth is unhindered, his mouth meets mine, firm lips with a soft tongue pressing between. I hesitate allowing him access, giving him something that for some reason seems so much more intimate than everything else he's done to me.

I feel myself weaken, allow myself to kiss him back and welcome his tongue dancing intimately with mine. I suddenly crave this connection, need to feel like there is something more, need to feel like there is a justification for all of these unexpected emotions and unequivocal acceptance of the situation I'm in. I turn myself over to it—to him—because it's easier to focus on him and the tenderness he's showing me than to focus on my captivity or the voyeur watching us, waiting to stake his claim someway, somehow.

He loosens his grip from my chin, his rough fingertips rasping across the line of my jaw. I moan softly into the kiss, tears welling in my closed eyes at the irony in the reverence of his touch for just a moment before the guilt starts to eat at me. I begin to question how I can turn myself over so easily to another man—regardless of circumstances, regardless of the bindings holding me hostage—when Anderson has been *it* for me for over fifteen years. I start to drown in the thought when I feel a finger trace the swollen flesh between my thighs.

I yelp, startled and unnerved that this person who I'm told likes to watch, now appears to like to touch too. And my head is so messed up with everything that I don't think properly, his unexpected touch pulls my thoughts and my mouth from our kiss. I try to scoot closer to the man in front of me. It's almost as if I'm looking toward the man who brought me here to protect me from the threat I feel of Marco at my back. A hand lands sharply on my ass in reprimand. This time the force is much harder than before and the sting is sharp and distinct beneath his resting palm.

Hands suddenly frame my face as my captor kisses me again, but this time with a commanding desperation. His tongue delves, teeth nip, and mouth takes more from me. All the while Marco slides his hands back and forth over my backside. I try and concentrate on the movement over my still singing flesh, but my mind is overwhelmed from the claim being staked on my mouth.

Marco's fingertips move—two fingers paralleling each other—sliding down the curve of my ass to the tops of my thighs. They stop and slide inward until I can feel them trace over the moisture at my entrance. My body tenses, my mind having trouble which sensation to focus on.

My captor relents his possession of my mouth, and I suck in a breath of air trying to gain some semblance of balance. And the few seconds I have to do just that are stolen when I feel the head of his dick press between my parted lips the same time as Marco slides his fingers into me. I gasp out at the feeling and his dick slips farther into my mouth predicated by his carnal groan from above me.

My mind flashes to the thoughts I had previously of biting him if he tried this. How he taunted me, told me I'd beg for this. His taste fills my mouth as he presses deeper into me, hitting the back of my throat before pulling slowly back out.

My captor's hand fists my hair, holding my head still as he fucks my mouth while Marco's hand grips the flesh on my hips and fingers me in a matching rhythm. My body rides this libidinous high as I'm worked into a frenzy, the sound of pleasure emanating from both men filling the room along with the slick sounds of my sex being worked.

I'm breathless, overwhelmed, and underequipped to process the onslaught of sensations wracking through my body. My thighs tremble above where my knees are pressed into the bed, and my hands are desperate for the freedom to grip his shaft. The men continue their ministrations, pleasure increasing and my body falling under the spell of unwanted desire. I feel him swell and harden to steel in my mouth, and he suddenly withdraws, the bed dipping as he drops down in front of me. His mouth on mine again momentarily as Marco's fingers stop moving but remain idly inside of me.

My captor pulls back from my lips again as I adjust my hips to try and ease the need anchoring me. I can feel his breath on my face as if he's staring at me, and I can't shake the feeling that he's trying to tell me something even though I can't see his eyes. He shifts, the bed sways, and his finger trails from my shoulder and down my spine in that way he has as he maneuvers himself behind me.

I suck in a breath, my conflicting emotions raging inside of me, and I can't help but tuck my hips forward as anticipation suffocates the air around me. His fingertip stops and presses at the top of my tailbone, and a low hum of approval sounds in the back of his throat. Feet shuffle, Marco's fingers withdraw from my wetness, and words are spoken softly between the two men that I wouldn't understand even if I could hear them.

Two hands grip either side of my hips, my breath quickening and possibilities flickering through my mind. He spreads me apart and cool air comingles with the pooling moisture. "You want this don't you, *bella Lilly*? Look at your pussy quiver and ass pucker in anticipation. Fuck that's sexy. Makes me want to claim every single part of you," he says as one hand releases my hip and his finger trails back down over every inch of skin to my clit and then back up.

I hear the click of a bottle and startle as I feel the cool liquid pour over me. My body vibrates with arousal and fear—of another thing that I've always wanted to try—and I bow my head and wait. I feel fingers spread the lubricant up and down the seam of my core and then stop. My breath shudders and my nipples tighten instantly when I feel the tip of his finger press against my tight rim and into me. My muscles fight to reject him and the slight discomfort his entrance brings, but he just holds still, allowing me to adjust.

"Ahhh," he sighs as I feel like my breath has been robbed. After a moment he starts to move his finger slowly in and out, soft noises of appreciation emanating from behind me as I talk myself into relaxing. "I need to prepare you, bella. Open you up. And then you're going to get fucked. Have you ever been filled? Have you ever felt two cocks moving inside of you? Rubbing against one another as they make you come?"

I moan out at the dark promise of his words and at the slight sting as he pulls out and pushes two fingers into me to stretch me farther. I'm just about used to the feeling when the head of his dick rests against the entrance to my sex, taunting me with possibilities of what's to come. He leaves it resting there—a tantalizing torture for me to crave—before he begins to move his fingers again at a faster pace.

My head hangs down, my hair tickling my cheeks as it falls over the blindfold, and I absorb everything that's being awakened within me. I'm not sure what I expected, but I don't feel much, and then when he thrusts his cock into my pussy and his fingers begin to move again, two worlds of sensations crash together. His forward movements push his fingers in farther and the hum in the back of my throat involuntarily comes out as my muscles begin to loosen and accept.

He rides me in a slow and steady cadence that allows me to feel every ridge of his crest as he slides in and back against my slick walls. I lose myself—my thoughts, my guilt, my resistance—in the calming rhythm of his body owning mine. My breasts jostle forward each time his hips connect with the backs of my thighs and urges the ache to burn a little stronger, a little deeper.

His other hand smooths across my ass, but it's the feel of a pointed tip of an object firm yet soft that pulls my mind from the haze of mounting pleasure. He runs the object slowly over one side of my buttocks and then rolls it across my lower back so I can feel the unmistakable shape of the plug before he continues down the other side. He then glides the point slowly up between my legs and around his cock and fingers buried within me, a taunting foreplay of what comes next.

My captor continues to trace imaginary lines with the plug over and over, my mind becoming so used to the feeling, the heightened awareness of its course that I begin to fall back under the rhythm of my building orgasm. And it's when I do this, when I allow myself to succumb to the barrage of sensation within caused by his skillful cock, that he pulls his fingers out and pushes the plug inside of me. Because it's a little larger, a little harder, it causes the abundance of nerves there to sing in resistance for a moment.

My body tenses at the lasting burn, earning me a tsk from him. "Relax. Don't fight it, bella. *Trust me.*"

My mind focuses on those words again as he stills his hips and presses the plug in even farther until it fits within my rim and my muscles flex around it. My eyes sting from the quick sear of pain, but before I can wriggle my hips away from him, his hands dig into the curves of my ass and squeeze possessively as he slams into me, the slap of skin on skin a mix with his guttural groan. I forget that there is someone else in the room, forget the threat to find pleasure and enjoy, because that option was a forgone conclusion the minute he thrust inside of me.

And this time as he works my pussy over and over, my muscles begin to clench around him and the overabundance of nerves stretched around the plug light everything on fire a little stronger, a lot more intense. The warmth begins to surge through my body, thoughts, desires, and pleasure—all colliding in a perfect storm of sensation that I've lost the fight to resist. My shoulders sag, my elbows give way, and my chest and shoulders press into the mattress beneath me, giving him one hundred percent control to manipulate my sex.

And even though I'd felt the buildup of my orgasm, when it hits me, when my body seizes with the catastrophic depths of pleasure that pulse through my core and reverberate through my every fiber, I'm stunned speechless at the unfettered intensity of it. My body writhes uncontrollably, my lips part with a moan, and goose bumps blanket my body despite the heat holding me hostage.

"So beautiful, so responsive," he murmurs as he stills within me and caresses the curve of my ass. I slowly reawaken from my post-orgasmic coma and recognize the unmistakable sounds of Marco stroking himself beside me. I'm immediately on alert, my synapses firing despite still being drugged from the orgasm's intoxication. The awareness of his presence, of the knowledge that he is here getting off watching us, leaves me feeling vulnerable, ashamed.

"Are you ready?"

My head jolts up at my captor's voice, unsure which of us he's speaking to. I exhale slowly, waiting in silent impatience as my captor withdraws from me. The sudden emptiness is unwelcome and unexpected, but I bite back the groan of disapproval because I have a feeling he is no longer the one in control, Marco is.

"What is your choice? *Entrambi sono la perfezione.*" His hands leave my skin, the plug still remaining, and I hear the floorboards creak as he steps back. His chuckle resonates in the room in a response I can't see. "As you wish," he says and I work a swallow down my throat as I wait to learn the ramifications of that statement.

I cry as my hips are grabbed roughly and jerked up in the air. I instinctively angle my head back to try and see what's happening—my mind so occupied on what's next, I forget the blindfold covering my eyes. I feel someone move between my parted legs, and my sight isn't needed to understand what happens next. I'm forced up on my elbows as a body slides beneath me and up the mattress, bare flesh grazing just barely against my hypersensitive skin. I suck in a breath as he shudders one out when my nipples slide over his chest as he positions himself. I feel tugging at my ankle restraints and then feel the tension ease the strain on my legs. I pull my legs in closer, relieved to have more freedom and find them framing the torso beneath me. I flex my hips, the plug slightly uncomfortable as it remains within me.

Who is beneath me and who is behind me?

My mind works furiously trying to calm myself as nerves hum and anxiety ratchets to new heights. I know what is going to happen next, have always wondered what it would be like, but now that I'm here in the moment, I'm nervous. I never figured I'd actually talk Anderson into trying this, and obviously, I never expected if I did get the chance that I'd be bound and blindfolded.

Chills dance up my spine as my breasts brush against the chest beneath me, and I still as hands frame my jaw. "Are you ready?" my captor murmurs into my ear. I sag in relief, thankful again that he is the one beneath me, the one near my face, because Marco unnerves me. I've formed a misconstrued trust with my captor, but in this situation filled with unknowns, I know he may have started all of this, but he has also kept his word to me thus far.

I exhale a shaky breath and nod subtly as I feel Marco brush against me from behind. "Bella, do you have any idea how gorgeous you look right now? How jealous your husband should be that I get to fuck you when you look like this? Nipples tight, pussy dripping, wax hardened, and my marks on your back? Does he know you need this? Need to be tested? Dominated? Filled? Used? Fucked within an inch of exhaustion?"

A strangled sound comes from my throat—part sob, part desperation—when he refers to Anderson. I don't want him mentioned, don't want to be reminded of the kindhearted man I am betraying. No, that I'm being *forced to betray*. My body vibrates for more, but my head begins to win the battle, the guilt returning full force. The tears well and my limbs tremble as his hands run down the sides of my torso, rough calluses against my smooth skin.

He slides his hands down to my hips and guides them forward before releasing one hand. I immediately feel the crest of his cock swipe over my clit, separating the flesh there, and positioning himself at my entrance. Marco's hands grab hold of my hips from behind, and slowly pushes me down so that my captor's cock fills me at an agonizingly slow pace. My body shudders at the sensation, nerves raked over, and swollen muscles unable to resist the re-ignition of desire. Fingers reach down and apply lubricant gently around where we are joined and then back up to where the plug still remains.

"Are you ready?" he whispers beneath me as his hands guide my shoulders forward, my breasts now pressed against his chest to give Marco better access.

The wings of panic begin to flutter anew, fear fanning it as I feel his fingers grip onto the base of the plug and begin to remove it. The mewling sound I make is involuntary, my heart thudding—that potent mixture of the unknown and the wanting to know messing with my head more than it already is.

The plug slips out and my whole body tenses when I feel a generous amount of lubricant applied. I suck in my breath, emotions warring, body anticipating, and ache intensifying while I sit in that suspended state of time between fingers leaving my skin and waiting for the next contact.

The head of his cock presses against my forbidden entrance, and Anderson flashes through my mind causing a sob to tear through my throat. This isn't how I want this. I mean, I want this—to try this—but with Anderson, my husband … not forced and …

My body tremors and the tears fall. I start to struggle away, start to try and fight against this, against him. My shout fills the room. Hands grip my shoulders and pull me tightly against my captor's chest. His arms hold me there, my hips wriggling—pleasure I don't want presenting itself as my clit moves against the length of his cock still within me.

"Don't fight us." His voice is a demand in my ear. "You want this. We want this." I resist again as Marco presses against my unrelenting muscles. "We're going to claim that virgin ass of yours. Going to fuck you, one hole for each of us. Going to make you realize just how good it feels to be that dirty little whore you want to be … you fight to deny."

I begin to shift again but this time it's because no matter how overwhelming the situation is—how much I don't want to be at the mercy of two men I can't even see—I'm dripping in moisture. My desire to continue more than evident as it slides out of me and over our connection.

I hold onto the inexplicable and misguided sense of trust that I feel with the man who began this whole bizarre situation. I grasp onto the now and not the why as Marco's dick pushes into me. The searing pain assaults me when he forces his head through the tight ring of unforgiving muscles.

My eyes water and I shout out at the indescribable pain. My body bucks in resistance as both men use their hands to hold me still.

"Hold on. Once his head's in, we'll let you adjust," he almost croons to me against the riot of noise filling my head. "Don't make me gag you," he warns when I don't stop.

I bite my lip to turn the shouts to whimpers, and I'm so focused on the threat of the gag that it takes me a moment to realize that the sting is dissipating. I even out my breathing as the rest of the pain fades and I feel fingers applying more lube. And then Marco ever so slowly starts to move. He pushes farther into me and the breath I've just evened out gets stolen.

The orgasm rips through me at a lightning fast pace. I don't have time to wonder if it's the million nerve endings hidden within the ring Marco just pulled on, or the idea of doing something others had always called taboo, or if it actually feels good because the intensity with which my release hits rivals no other climax I've ever experienced.

I couldn't fight the pleasure that violently rips through me even if I wanted to. My legs clench into the hips they frame, my feet curl, my mouth falls open, but I'm so overwhelmed with the overabundance of different sensations I can't utter a sound. My breath is held hostage by the pleasure edged with pain, and I don't even realize it, don't even attempt to find it, as my pussy clamps down and muscles pulse rhythmically around both cocks filling me. And I don't know if it's being stretched—filled so incredibly full—but my orgasm rages on, my body tremoring and head lost to the orgasmic haze.

And then they start to move.

My breath comes back. The twinge of pain is still there, but my adrenaline is on such a high, the ache that should be sated is already ratcheting upwards. I think I moan, I don't even know because all I smell is peppermint, all I feel is pleasure, all I want is more.

The push and pull of one dick moving in while the other moves out. The feel of them rubbing together through the thin interior wall between them. One pair of hands on my hips, the other holding me down. The pants of exertion and slick sound of lubed flesh being worked. Every single thing assaults my senses, drags me under yet has me on edge, waiting, wanting, willing to come again.

To take what I want for the first time in so very long.

Anderson flickers through my mind, and I push him away. I can't have him here right now, can't think of him while feeling all of this, because then I'd have to admit that this is what I want.

This is what I need.

That this is that little bit more …

Chapter 6

MY HEAD LOLLS forward, my forehead against my captor's shoulder as his arms continue to hold and guide me. My body still simmers, still burns for more, but I don't know how much more I can handle. I'm exhausted: physically, mentally, sexually. For a girl used to one orgasm at a time, my body can't come any more.

I think the men realize this, but they don't relent as they chase their own releases.

Time lapses and positions change.

Murmured words are spoken from my captor.

Fingers grip my hips.

Grunts and the sound of flesh hitting flesh.

Moans of release.

Sleep comes without thought.

The smell of peppermint awakes me way too soon.

I'm allowed to use the facilities.

Never alone.

Drink of water offered.

Refastened to bed for another round to begin.
On my back.
This time just Marco.
Still silent.
Presence still dominating the room.
The only connection is where our bodies join.
First him.
Then my captor.
Pleading with them to stop.
Can't take anymore.
Saying Anderson's name over and over.
Focusing on the peppermint.
Not the continuous onslaught of sensation.
Feeling like a rag doll.
But the orgasms still come.
Drowning in the unwelcome pleasure.
Body traitorous.
Mind escaping.
Drinking more water.
Wishing for the chocolate covered strawberries.

Head becoming fuzzy. Just like walking back to the hotel.

Darkness closing in.
Feeling free. Weightless, cradled.
Peppermint again.
Cool Air. Bright lights.
The ding of an elevator.

"My girlfriend." My captor's voice. A soft, knowing chuckle. "Silly American pride made her think she could handle our vino." The warmth of a kiss pressed to my forehead. Polite laughter. Murmured good lucks.

The ding of the elevator.

Sinking into softness.
Cocooned in blankets.
“Ora sei libero,” murmured against my ear.
Blackness.

Chapter 7

I SHIFT RESTLESSLY in the bed, my head groggy and body aching. I roll over onto my stomach and feel a crackling over my chest. My mind snaps awake with awareness and I bolt up in the bed with a groan. The light hits my eyes and I raise an arm to shield them from its harsh rays. My heart pounds and once my eyes can adjust, they dart frantically around the room.

My hotel room.

I immediately grab the bedding and hold it to my chest in a ridiculous form of protection from the silence and the unknown. It takes me a second to catch my breath, to even out my pulse, and to really believe that I'm here.

Alone.

My mind rifles over everything, memories and sensations crashing together like a demolition derby. I immediately curl into myself—knees to chest—arms protective around them. And if I didn't feel the ache in my limbs, the tenderness between my thighs, the wax dried on my chest, and the bites of pain along my back, I'd swear it was all a dream. The abduction, being fucked every which way imaginable, and then *nothing* until waking up here in my bed in my hotel room.

I choke back at the bile that rises in my throat when those images materialize into actuality. When I realize that what I'd hoped was a dream is actually reality. My body protests but I'm off the bed in a heartbeat and running into the bathroom. I can't turn the shower on quick enough, can't wait to rid my body of the reminders that still brand me: the feel of his fingers, his scent mixed with mine, the dried wax, the salt on my skin. Mentally scattered, I step into the tiled enclosure without thought. The shock of cold jolts my mind to the present, my voice crying out and echoing over the tiles is a disconcerting sound.

Why didn't I yell for help yesterday when I was being held against my will, but I cry out now because of something as menial as a cold shower?

The question circles in my mind, my body sagging against the chilled wall behind me, my conscience trying to disengage from the facts. The guilt. The doubts. The truths.

Why didn't I fight harder, resist more? Did I allow everything to happen? Is this on me?

The temperature of the water heats in an instant. Cold to hot. Frigid to inviting. Was that me yesterday? Resistant and unwilling, then accepting and compliant on a turn of a dime.

I choke back the bile as the thought hits me. As I question myself and what I should or shouldn't have done. Of the things I found pleasure in.

"Oh God." The words tumbling from my mouth are like a repeated mantra as I stand mid-stream and let the scalding water burn lines down my skin. I grab the bar of soap with trembling hands and begin to scrub my body with vigor. The steam suffocates the small bathroom but is no match for the weight smothering my soul.

I reduce the bar to a sliver and immediately open another package of the cheap hotel soap and begin anew until my skin is pink, raw, and abraded. *But it's not enough.* I'm still dirty, still tarnished—inside and out. I take my fingers and lather them with soap and slide them between my legs and inside of me, trying to wash every trace of him away as best as I can. I move in a frenzy. My swollen, torn skin stings when the soap hits it, but it doesn't matter. I can't seem to cleanse the claim he staked.

Tears fall. My body shivers. I open my mouth to let the scalding water fill it and burn my palate. I can't seem to erase the taste of his kiss or the feeling of his dick sliding over my tongue. I start to gag at the thought, water spraying everywhere as I choke and cough and attempt to draw in air.

And I don't know how long I stand there, the hot water burning welts on my skin, but I don't care. I welcome the forced focus on the pain, the cleansing of my flesh, because it's easier to concentrate on that rather than the doubts and questions and thoughts that overwhelm my mind.

The ones I'm afraid to look at closer, find answers to.

I stumble out of the shower after some time. I go through the haphazard mechanics of sliding on the hotel provided robe and pull it as tight as I can around me. I'm freezing. The muggy Italian weather permeates the room, but I'm so very cold. I walk the short distance to the bed, crawl back into it, teeth chattering and body exhausted.

But it's now that I'm physically cleansed—that my eyes are closed and body is sinking into the mattress—that I can hear the cars on the street below and the sound of the vacuum in another room nearby. My throat constricts momentarily.

Is that where they had me? Held me against my will just a few rooms down from this one? I try to process the possibilities. I have no idea, and the panic hits me full force again, the thought an unexpected blindside. Was I really being held so close to here? Could I have screamed and stopped the course of emotional destruction I now find myself on. My heart thunders and hands tremble.

I squeeze my eyes shut and force myself to focus on my surroundings. Everything seems the same as it did yesterday … or the day before yesterday. I fixate on that. On the normalcy of everything, hoping my mind can shut down for a few moments. I have no idea how much time has passed but it all seems the same, and yet every single thing in me has shifted, been forever changed.

I finally allow my mind to go there, to try and process what the hell happened: the whys, the what-fors, the answers for some reason I know I'll never find. I reach down out of habit to twist my bracelet, my small form of comfort amidst this maelstrom and touch bare skin. I look down to my wrist, thoughts warring when I find my favorite piece of jewelry gone.

The anxiety returns as my mind tries to recall if I had it on last night. If I lost it during everything that happened. I urge my mind to fire, to break through the fuzzy memories, but the furthest I can recall is waking up bound and blindfolded.

I start to get up, want to look for it, needing that reminder of my family—my boys—to hold on to right now, but I stop when my eyes catch a glimpse of the faint red lines ringing my wrists. I pull them in close to my chest and rub them, my mind losing focus on what I was going to do. After a moment lost in thought, I hold them out and stare at them again. The funny thing is I know that when the marks fade, I'll still feel them—somehow, someway—because what was done to me will be etched in my soul forever.

The question is, is it a nightmare or a memory?

I think of a kidnapper I trusted in some inexplicable, screwed-up way, who tried to protect me, praised me, showed me an unexpected and sporadic tenderness. How does someone wrap their head around that? Kidnapping, drugging, and restraints are in no way consensual, so how did he make me feel like it was my choice?

My thoughts flicker to Marco, the person who said nothing but whose presence owned the room with his mere silence. His cold demeanor and lack of tactility from his place at the end of the bed such a stark contrast to my kidnapper's. The mysterious man who sat there watching without so much as a word, but who took something from me I've never given anybody else.

And then I think of Anderson. The sob catches in my throat as I focus on the betrayal and infidelity until the guilt wreaks havoc in my psyche. I scramble off the bed to the dresser where my cell phone lies and grab it like a life line, not understanding why this wasn't my first thought when I woke up. There are ten texts from him asking if I'm alright, to call him back, that he's going into more meetings. My hands grip it tightly, knuckles turning white as the tears return and course down my cheeks. I welcome the feeling, the shedding of emotions that weigh heavy.

Do I tell him? Do I go home and act like this never happened? Carry on life as usual all the while I'm reeling inside with … what? What exactly am I feeling?

Relieved.

Confused.

Sated.

"Oh God," I whisper my mantra into the room. Memories stain my mind and unease reigns in my soul. One hand grips my phone—the platinum of my wedding ring clicking against it—while the other lifts involuntarily to cover my lips. I sag onto the bed and succumb to the onslaught of emotions I'm not quite sure how to handle.

I wasn't harmed. I was put back in my hotel room. Is anyone going to really believe I was abducted, sexually manipulated, and released physically uninjured? I blow out a breath, my fingers on my lips now beginning to tremble. I'm in a foreign country. Alone. I've just washed all traces of them from me without thought. If

I went to the authorities, would they really believe me?

Indecision wars as time passes, the discomfort with each movement a subtle reminder of everything. Shadows shift across the room as the day wages on.

I cry when my cell rings. The sound seems so foreign in my echo chamber of thoughts. I fumble the phone momentarily, my hand sore from unconsciously gripping it all this time, and look down to see who's calling.

Anderson.

I stare wide-eyed at his picture on the screen for what seems like forever but is really only two rings. The rush of blood in my ears drowns out the ringtone as I swallow over the lump in my throat. I know it's only seconds that pass, but it feels like hours that I stare at the screen. Indecision wars. And then once I choose to answer, I can't get the phone to my ear quick enough.

"Hello?" I'm already sobbing the words out, breath hitching, desperation echoing in my voice.

"Lil? Lil, what's wrong?" And it's his voice—concern, comfort, everything—that undoes me. *Unravels me.* Hits me like a sucker punch to the gut. I can't catch my breath fast enough, can't speak, because I'm overwhelmed by the truths I'm finally ready to face. To accept.

This man is my everything.

He has been for so long, how in the hell could I think of wanting anyone else? Sure sex might be a little boring sometimes, it might be predictable or scheduled to minimize the off chance of being interrupted by the boys, but is that really on him? Is the rut we've fallen into all his fault?

I've become complacent. I've taken his place beside me for granted. Aren't I just as much to blame for this as he is? Haven't I stopped putting our marriage first just as he has too?

"Lil, answer me! You're scaring the shit out of me!" The urgency and fear in his voice comes through the connection loud and clear, jolting me from my thoughts. I can visualize him pacing in front of his desk, one hand on the phone, the other shoving through his hair.

"I'm okay," I manage. "I'm okay." I suck in a breath and will myself to calm down because I can't answer the questions he's going to ask, and the more composed I am, the less insistent he'll be for a response.

"What's going on?" His voice softens some but concern is still prominent.

"I just—I just miss you." I hiccup the words, biting my knuckles to prevent another sob from falling out as the die is cast.

I can't tell him.

I know I'm sealing my fate to Hell by lying, but I can't bring myself to do it. I can't shatter that innate male instinct he has to protect me. I'm okay. I'm unharmed. The damage done to me is far less than what it would do to him. He would never look at me the same. His empathy—one of the reasons I fell in love with him in the first place—would lead him to coddle and handle me with kid gloves. The fact that everything happened—he'd look at it as a failure as a man, as a husband to protect me—would gnaw at him until he self-destructed.

Do I destroy the man I love to assuage my own

guilt?

"Hun, you okay? Why are you crying?"

His words break through my thoughts. The tone of his voice almost shatters my resolve. The confession is on my tongue, but I close my eyes and force a swallow. Internalize my own pain to prevent his.

"Nothing. I just got sick and … and I can't wait to come home. I miss you, the boys … home." I press my thumb over the speaker on the phone so he can't hear the telling sound of my hitching breath.

"Are you sure, Lil? You don't sound good." I'm silent. I don't trust my voice just yet. "I'm flying out there."

"No!" The words are out of my mouth, his declaration causing mine. A desperate plea. My epiphany so simple yet so daunting all at the same time. He can't come see me because I need today and the next to compose myself, to absorb everything that happened, heal some of the physical marks, figure how to cope with the emotional reminders. To allow me the time to accept this experience has changed me and figure out the words to tell him I need a little more out of our sex life: experimenting, dominance, variation. To be able to express our marriage or him being enough for me isn't the problem, no, but my need for him to give me something more in the bedroom is.

The answer I need to figure out though is, will that admission hurt him as much as me telling him about what happened? Blindside him when he thought we were happy and I'm far from it? Make him feel inadequate?

"I'll be fine. I'm going to change my flight to tomorrow sometime and come home early." I unfist my hands gripping the comforter and hold my breath waiting for his response.

"Lil, I don't like—"

"I'm fine. I'll be fine." I stumble over the words, but I'm not sure if I'm trying to reassure him or me. "I've already looked at flights … I was just picking up the phone to call you and tell you."

One lie upon another.

What a tangled web we weave.

"Lil …" His voice trails off, the unasked question falling into its silence.

I worry my bottom lip between my teeth and wait for the questions, the inkling that he knows what happened—guilt screaming loud like my own personal tell-tale heart.

"I'm sorry," he finally says. "I should have told work to go to Hell. I should be there with you, taking care of you." I can hear the regret, the evidence that he's beating himself up over choosing his career over us. My God, I can't imagine what he'd be like if he really knew what happened.

"Ander—"

"Lil …" He blows out a long breath. "We need to … we'll talk when you get home, okay? Text me your flight info when you change it and … get some rest, okay?"

"Mmm-hmm."

"Love you."

"Love you too."

The line disconnects but I hold the phone to my ear for I don't know how long, my decision warring against my rationality. And the only thing that breaks the endless spiral of guilt is when the words float through my mind like a distant memory.

Ora sei libero.

I can hear his voice say them, feel his breath heat my lips, but can't remember anything else he said. I lower the phone from my ear and type the words in. My hands shake and I misspell them a few times but finally Google gives me the answer I am looking for.

I blink my eyes a couple of times and shake my head in what has to be misunderstanding of the words, their meaning.

You are now free.

Chapter 8

"WHAT'S BROUGHT ALL of this on?" The look of confusion on Anderson's face worries me. Is he going to tell me no? Again? Reject me and my even-keeled plea?

You are now free.

I hiccup back the guilt—a heavy presence wanting to tell the truth—and lower my eyes to stare at my hands fiddling in my lap. Thoughts flash through my mind of earlier. The relief I felt seeing Anderson at the airport. The unfettered love that coursed through me when he wrapped his arms around me. The calm that came over me mixed with the feeling of safety, comfort, acceptance, loyalty with just the smell of his cologne and security of his arms. How I cried like a baby in the middle of the terminal as he held me, whispering reassurances to calm the outpouring of emotions he didn't understand.

Driving home. Rapid-fire chat about what the other has been doing. And I tell him everything … everything but what I want to tell him the most. Apologies from him. How he screwed up, should have told work to take a hike, and put me first, put us first. How he's thought about his priorities and where he's gone wrong. How being all alone for a week—with nothing but your own thoughts—will do that to you.

I accept his apologies and then make my own—for the same reasons and for ones he'll never have a clue about. The tears fall. Hope renews and murmured promises are made for the changes that need to be made.

And then we come home to a lonely house. My boys won't be back from my mom's for another day. Panic becomes hysteria; the thoughts I had those first few minutes after I woke up blindfolded flood back with a vengeance. I start to ramble, tell Anderson we need to get the boys now. Right now. I need to see them, kiss them, inhale their little boy scent as I hold them tight.

I begin to cry. Think of what I could have lost. Anderson calms me down, tells me travel arrangements are already made for tomorrow and too late to cancel. That we need to enjoy the one night we have together for our anniversary. Make the most of it. Start proving everything we just said to each other in the car.

I calm myself and stare at him for a moment before taking a deep breath to say what it feels has taken me a lifetime to confess. I ask that he doesn't speak until I finish. I tell him I love him more than anything. I express to him that in losing the us that we once were, we also lost that spark in the bedroom. The want to please the other, the desire to be spontaneous, try new things, step outside of the box.

He nods his head at me, granting my request for silence as I gather my last thoughts together. The feelings evoked from the hotel room flood back tenfold and crowd the room around us, giving me the courage I need to finish what I need to say. We sit like this for some time, no words exchanged but our eyes speaking volumes: willingness and trust. Acceptance and understanding. But for some reason, the silence we sit in doesn't seem so lonely anymore. It's filled with a spark of what's been missing for some time.

And so I add fuel to the spark, hoping it catches fire.

You are now free.

Instead of hinting at things I want as I have in the past, I flat out tell him. New positions, toys, anal, sex-swings, light bondage. Nothing earth-shattering to many these days but life changing for me. I say each sentence, pay particular attention to each word, and watch his reactions. I reassure that I love him, that I'm happy, that he's more than enough, but that with age, with confidence, I want more. I need more.

And I want to find that more in him, with him.

I exhale loudly into the silence I've asked for. My nerves hum and I jostle my knee as we continue to stare at each other, his silence a slow torture to me. I need him to respond, need him to tell me that I'm not asking for too much. That he can give this to me.

But he doesn't say a word but rather stands up and disappears from my sight. I bite my lip to fight the tears that threaten and the predicted rejection that lodges in my throat. It doesn't matter how many times he rebuffs me, each time is just as devastating as the first. I squeeze my eyes, the gamut of emotions overtaking me as I hold everything in: Anderson's dismissal after our promises earlier, the guilt and shame riding a close second.

The bed shifts and Anderson places his hand on my thigh, squeezing it when I refuse to open my eyes. "Lil?" There is a gentleness to his tone that pulls on so many things within me that I open my eyes to meet his. He reaches out and frames my face—his thumb brushing away the lone tear I couldn't contain—and the tenderness in his touch almost makes me lose my hold on the reminder of them.

He repeats his question again, pulling me from my thoughts. "What brought all this on now? Is it because of these?"

He bends over to pick something off the floor beside the bed and I'm surprised to see the box from my closet. I stare at him as he takes the lid from it and sets the container between us. My eyes flicker back and forth, trying to gauge the expression on his face juxtaposed to the quiet ache that the sight of some of the toys create.

Because now I know just how much they can enhance my pleasure.

My cheeks stain red as I stare at them and silently, guiltily recalling those sensations while Anderson watches me—the weight of his stare as he waits for an answer flusters me.

"Yes. No. Yes …" I blow out an exasperated breath and look up from where I am fiddling with my fingers to meet the clear brown of his eyes. "I just …" My voice trails off for the first time, losing my confidence. I take a moment and when I look down and see the invisible lines on my wrists, they give me what I need to be honest. "This time apart has made me realize how much I love you, but that I've been unhappy, resentful … that for some time, I've been jealous of the old 'us' and I don't want to be that way anymore. That's a horrible place to be. We've let life get in the way … put everything else first, and I think this—discovering new things together—will make us find that trust in one another, rekindle what we used to have." I shrug, tears welling in my eyes. "I don't know. At first I thought the toys might help … but now ... All I know, all I care about is that I miss … us."

Anderson gives me a measured nod followed by a full blown smirk. The one that fifteen years ago captured my heart when he walked past me in his football uniform during lunch in the quad.

"After this week, us being apart because of work, once again … I realized I miss us too," he says with a nod of his head. He reaches in the box and moves items around with an obvious unease, but at least he's looking. He quiets for a moment before looking up and meeting my eyes. "I've been stubborn. I've been so wrapped up thinking with my ego and not my dick that I've completely missed the whole point." I suppress the burgeoning hope I feel, afraid to believe too quickly that Anderson has finally heard me. "Without you here, I realized that it's lonely as hell … and that I need to stop and listen to you sometimes, really hear the words you're saying. And you've been saying that these toys don't mean that I'm not enough, but rather you just want a little more variety."

I close my eyes, the tears leaking out because he finally gets it. I hiccup back a sob as relief finally finds its place within me.

With eyes steadfast on mine, he leans in and closes the distance between us. "You know what I think?" he says, an eyebrow raising and desire darkening in his eyes.

"Hmm?" I can't speak. It's been forever since I have seen that cocky look on his face and in a sense, he just gave me my answer without saying a word.

"I think that we should start with this." Anderson holds up a Lelo vibrator from the box and I groan out softly at the thought. "Well then, it's settled. I'm going to go grab a quick shower, and when I come back into the bedroom, you better be on the bed. Naked." He presses a kiss against my lips. "And ready to get fucked."

I startle my head back to look at him, the Anderson from fifteen years ago looking back at me. "So, you'll …"

"Five minutes." It's all he says as he stands up and starts to walk from the room, my pulse quickening, and the tingling that's been gone for so long when it comes to Anderson rushes back like a flash flood. My eyes track him as he pulls his shirt off on his way toward the bathroom. Disbelief and desire surging within me.

He passes through the doorway, stops, and turns around. "Hey, you never told me, did you get my anniversary present?"

My fingers still on my blouse where they are unbuttoning, and the chocolate covered strawberries flash through my head along with the unopened card I couldn't bring myself to read because of the guilt. "Yes, thank you," I gush, a little too fervently, before controlling my emotions so he doesn't know I'm lying. "I forgot when you called to tell you … they were so satisfying. Just what I needed."

He chokes out a cough, covering his mouth to physically stifle the violence of it.

"Hun, are you okay?" I begin to scoot off the end of the bed to help him but he just holds his hand up to stop me.

After a moment, he recovers and angles his head to the side, staring at me with confusion etching his features. "*Just what you needed?*" The inquiry in his voice has me explaining further.

"Yeah. The chocolate covered strawberries … *so delicious*."

"I didn't send you … they … those were courtesy of the hotel for our anniversary." Anderson stumbles over the words, bewilderment etching his features.

Now it's my turn to be confused. I shift my eyes back and forth as I try to figure out what he's talking about. "Huh …"

"Nothing else came to the room?"

"No … was it … I wasn't there much. Maybe …" I don't finish my thought, worried my excuses may tell too much and that maybe something was delivered while I was being held against my will.

"Hmpf," he says with a nonchalant shrug that contradicts the beseeching look in his eyes. His tongue darts out to lick his lips, and he just stares at me a bit longer before shaking his head in an amused defeat.

"What was it?" Now I'm curious. His conflicting posture and demeanor have me wanting to know what I'm going to miss out on.

"No worries." He smirks. "It … it definitely wasn't chocolate covered strawberries." He chuckles with a shake of his head.

I go to ask for more of an explanation but the look in his eyes stop me as he stalks towards me in a predatory manner "I guess I'll just have to make it up to you. Make sure I'm just what you need." He leans down and presses a kiss to my mouth, tongue delving between my lips to dance intimately with mine. And just as abruptly as he started the kiss, he turns and heads back in to the bathroom, throwing, "Five minutes and counting," over his shoulder.

I stare at the now empty doorway, my heart swollen with love, and my conscience a little lighter. Wow. I'm kind of in a state of disbelief. Over his apologies, his revelations, his acceptance of wanting more.

I pull my shirt over my head and unfasten my bra as I digest it all. I flop back on the bed and laugh aloud. *Our tenth wedding anniversary.* Who would have thought that not being together might have been the best thing to help us find each other again. Completely fucked up, but incredibly true.

I close my eyes for a moment. Images I never saw but can't erase run through my mind. I startle when the phone on the bed rings. It's Anderson's, and I never pick it up. I usually just look at it and then tell him who called so that he knows.

I reach out for it and sit up when I see the phone number. The Italian country code. My mind immediately thinks the hotel is calling because they found whatever gift Anderson sent me.

"Hello?"

"Ciao. This is the Mauro from Hotel Mulino di Firenze."

"Hi, yes. What can I do for you?" I ask, toeing off my shoes as I wait for the response.

"You recently stayed with us in our presidential suite, *si?*"

"Yes but not in the—"

"We found a bracelet under the bed when the room was cleaned that we think belongs to you."

"Bracelet?" Relief flows through me. I completely forgot about my bracelet, my mind so overwhelmed with processing the last seventy-two hours. But now that I'm reminded, I'm relieved they found it. Now I don't have to worry about having to explain to Anderson that I lost it. "Thank you so much … but … uh … I was in room two hundred something, not in the Presidential suite?"

"Oh, I'm sorry. I must have called the wrong number then. Let me—"

"I did lose a bracelet. Just, I didn't have a suite," I quickly correct him, thinking the language difference might be the problem in understanding, desperate to get my bracelet back.

"Scuzi … let me check." The line is silent for a moment, filled only with the click of a keyboard. "No, I'm sorry. The bracelet was most definitely found in the suite and it does have this phone number as the occupant …"

My pulse begins to race as adrenaline starts to

surge and awareness begins to break through the haze.

I hear more typing. "… ah yes, here it is. This is the correct number for Marco, si?"

"Yes," I whisper into my husband's telephone. *Marco's telephone.* The hotel clerk's voice now a distant sound in my ear.

My mind fires to process.

Trust me.

His words from his text flicker through my mind. He wasn't talking about our relationship. He was warning me, preparing me, informing me of what was going to happen. I try to grasp everything.

Try to understand the magnitude of what has happened.

Accept that fact that he's already given me everything I just asked him for.

Already given me *just what I needed.*

I guess I received my anniversary gift from Anderson after all.

About the Author

New York Times and USA Today Bestselling author K. Bromberg is that reserved woman sitting in the corner who has you all fooled about the wild child inside of her—the one she lets out every time her fingertips touch the computer keyboard.

K. lives in Southern California with her husband and three children. When she needs a break from the daily chaos of her life, you can most likely find her on the treadmill or with Kindle in hand, devouring the pages of a good, saucy book.

On a whim, K. Bromberg decided to try her hand at this writing thing. Her debut novels, Driven, Fueled, and Crashed of *The Driven Trilogy* were well received and went on to become multi-platform bestsellers as well as landing on the New York Times and USA Today lists. She is currently working on two stand alones, Slow Burn and Sweet Ache, as well as Raced and an untitled novella to the Driven Series.

Made in the USA
San Bernardino, CA
09 October 2014